My dear mouse friends,

Have I ever told you how much I love science fiction? I've always wanted to write incredible adventures set in another dimension, but I've never believed that parallel universes exist . . . until now!

That's because my good friend Professor Paws von Volt, the brilliant, secretive scientist, has just made an incredible discovery. Thanks to some mousetropic calculations, he determined that there are many different dimensions in time and space, where anything could be possible.

The professor's work inspired me to write this science fiction adventure in which my family and I travel through space in search of new worlds. We're a fabumouse crew: the spacemice!

I hope you enjoy this intergalactic adventure!

Geronimo Stilton

PROFESSOR
PAWS VON VOLT

THE SPACEMICE

GERONIMO STILTONIX
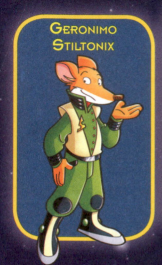

TRAP STILTONIX

THEA STILTONIX

GRANDFATHER WILLIAM STILTONIX

ROBOTIX

BENJAMIN STILTONIX AND BUGSY WUGSY
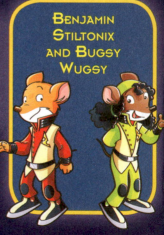

Geronimo Stilton

SPACEMICE

PIRATE SPACECAT ATTACK

Scholastic Inc.

Published by Scholastic Inc., *Publishers since 1920,* 557 Broadway, New York, NY 10012. SCHOLASTIC and associated logos are trademarks and/or registered trademarks of Scholastic Inc.

Stilton is the name of a famous English cheese. It is a registered trademark of the Stilton Cheese Makers' Association. For more information, go to www.stiltoncheese.com.

This book is a work of fiction. Names, characters, places, and incidents are either the product of the author's imagination or are used fictitiously, and any resemblance to actual persons, living or dead, business establishments, events, or locales is entirely coincidental.

ISBN 978-1-338-08860-1

Text by Geronimo Stilton
Original title *Sfida stellare all'ultimo baffo*
Cover by Flavio Ferron
Illustrations by Giuseppe Facciotto (design) and Daniele Verzini (color)
Graphics by Michela Battaglin

Special thanks to AnnMarie Anderson
Translated by Anna Pizzelli
Interior design by Kevin Callahan / BNGO Books
10 9 8 7 6 5 4 3 2 1   17 18 19 20 21

Printed in the U.S.A.   40
First printing 2017

In the darkness of the farthest galaxy in time and space is a spaceship inhabited exclusively by mice.

This fabumouse vessel is called the **MouseStar 1**, and I am its captain!

I am Geronimo Stiltonix, a somewhat accident-prone mouse who (to tell you the truth) would rather be writing novels than steering a spaceship.

But for now, my adventurous family and I are busy traveling around the universe on exciting intergalactic missions.

THIS IS THE LATEST ADVENTURE OF THE SPACEMICE!

Super-mega-cosmically Late!

It all started one quiet morning aboard the **mousestar 1**, the most mouserific spaceship in the universe. I was asleep, dreaming a wonderful dream: My book, *The Spacemouse's Guide to the Galaxy*, was receiving the prestigious *Intergalactic Literature Award*!

I stood on the stage as aliens from every corner of the solar system clapped and **SHOOK** their antennae in my **honor** . . .

Galactic Gorgonzola, my whiskers were **TREMBLING** with happiness!

The head judge was walking toward me with the award. I extended my paw to accept it, when—

Zzz . . . Zzz . . . Zzz . . .

Beep! Beeeep! Beeeep!
Beep! Beeeep! Beeeep!
Beep! Beeeep! Beeeep!
Beep! Beeeep! Beeeep!

I woke to the sound of my blaring alarm clock. Unfortunately, it wasn't the head judge standing in front of me. Instead, it was **Assistatrix**, my personal assistant robot.

"Good morning, Captain!" Assistatrix

exclaimed. It is time to get up! "It is ten twenty-seven INTERGALACTIC TIME."

"You couldn't have waited five more minutes?" I mumbled irritably. "I was in the middle of the BEST dream . . . Martian mozzarella! It's already ten twenty-seven ?!"

"Well, it is now ten twenty-eight, to be

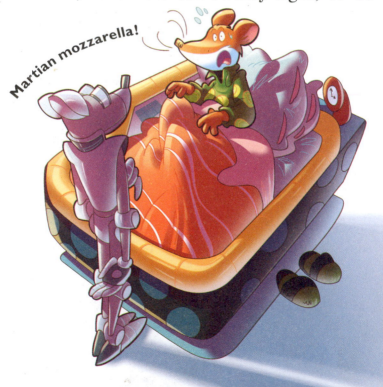

Martian mozzarella!

exact," Assistatrix replied. "It's time to —"

"**Get up!**" I squeaked. "I know! But you were supposed to wake me at eight! What happened?"

"Hologramix gave me the order to **reset** your alarm clock," Assistatrix replied.

"**HOLOGRAMIX** gave you an order?" I asked, surprised. "Since when is the ship's computer giving you orders?! The last time I checked, I was the captain."

Oops, I almost forgot to introduce myself! My name is Stiltonix, **Geronimo Stiltonix**, and I am the captain of the *MouseStar 1*. And that morning I was **SUPER-MEGA-COSMICALLY** late!

"Assistatrix, get my breakfast, please."

I **ran** to my closet. I had to get dressed!

WHERE'S MY UNIFORM?

My automated STYLIST greeted me when I opened my closet door.

"Good morning, Trap!"

Mousey meteorites, had I heard that correctly?

"Um . . . EXCUSE ME," I said. "What did you call me?"

"Trap Stiltonix!" the stylist replied.

"But my name isn't Trap!" I squeaked, confused. "Trap is my cousin!"

"Ha, ha, ha!" my stylist chuckled. "You're so funny. You always want to joke around!"

Joke around? What was my stylist SQUEAKING about?

"But I'm the captain of this ship," I

protested. "My name is Geron —"

Before I could finish, the stylist handed me a **uniform**.

"Enough *JOKING*!" my stylist ordered. "Here is your uniform. Now get dressed!"

I was **SUPER-MEGA-COSMICALLY** late, so I didn't have time to argue. Instead, I slipped one paw in one leg of the uniform and

Here is your uniform, Trap!

But I'm not Trap!

another in the arm . . . but the uniform was ENORMOUSE!

HOLEY CRATERS, it wasn't my uniform. It was my cousin Trap's!

"This isn't mine," I said quickly. "Where's my captain's uniform?"

"You would love to be the captain, wouldn't you?" my stylist replied, sounding annoyed.

"I am the captain!" I squeaked in frustration. What in the name of space cheese was going on?

"Ha, ha, ha!" the stylist chuckled. "You're such a jokester, Trap. But enough now. It's time to get dressed!"

At that moment, Assistatrix returned with my breakfast.

"Here you are, Captain!"

"Finally, good news!" I cheered. But a

second later I **smelled** a strange odor. "What is this?" I asked as I stirred the **STRANGE** greenish liquid in the bowl Assistatrix had delivered.

M-motor oil?!

"It's your **MOTOR OIL**, Captain!" the robot replied.

"M-motor oil?!" I exclaimed. "What are you squeaking about? I *always* have a cup of hot cheese in the morning!"

"**Not today, Captain!**" Assistatrix said.

"Oh, I get it!" I said with a laugh. "This is all a big joke. You're **kidding** me, right? Is today Furry Fool's Day?"

"No, this is not a *joke*," Assistatrix

replied. "The menu I received today from Hologramix is quite clear: Your breakfast is **motor oil**."

GALACTIC GORGONZOLA! What was going on? Since when did Hologramix choose my breakfast?

"Please excuse me, but I really have to **GO** now," Assistatrix said. Before I could squeak a word, my **PERSONAL ASSISTANT ROBOT** turned around and left.

I have to go now!

WHIRR

B-but . . .

WHAT ARE YOU DOING HERE, CAPTAIN?

I decided to head straight to the **control room**. I had to figure out what was going on! I hurried to the LIFTRIX. Then I stepped inside and pressed the button for the control room. But instead of whisking me **UP**, a powerful jet of air pushed me **DOWN**!

From the Encyclopedia Galactica
LiFTRIX

The liftrix is the fastest and most comfortable way to move around inside a spaceship. It's a glass tube that sucks up the passenger in a strong blast of air, carrying the spacemouse to the requested level of the ship.

Stinky space cheese, where was the liftrix taking me? A chill ran down my tail. Then, suddenly:

Boom!

I landed in something soft but stinky. It was a mountain of **dirty** clothes! I was in the **laundry room**!

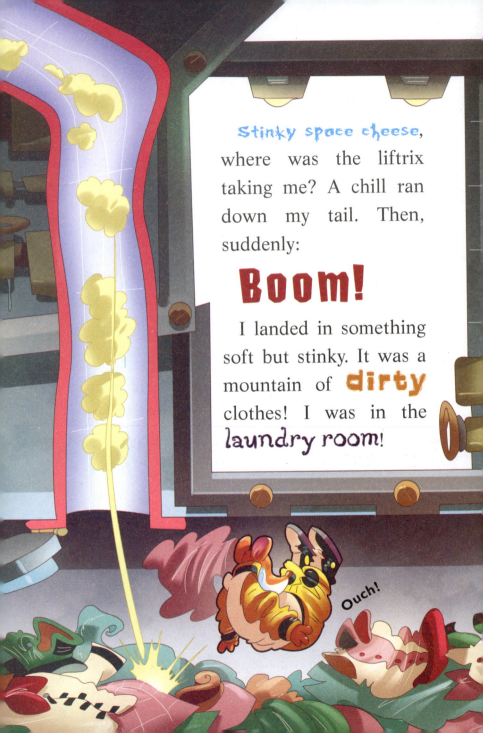

Ouch!

I tried to get up, but instead felt my fur being **pulled** toward a giant galactic washing machine.

Slurp . . . Blurp . . . Vrooooom!

The machine was *sucking up* all the dirty clothes, and I was next! *MARTIAN MOZZARELLA!* I squeezed my eyes shut, preparing for the worst . . . when someone suddenly grabbed me by the **PAW** and dragged me away from the washing machine.

I opened my eyes to see **Robotix**, the *MouseStar 1*'s multipurpose robot.

"Captain, what are you doing here?" Robotix asked. "Everyone is waiting for you in the control room! The ship is experiencing some technical problems."

"Yes, I noticed!" I replied. "My **ALARM CLOCK** went off late, my stylist handed me the wrong uniform, I had **MOTOR OIL** for breakfast, and the liftrix tossed me down here instead of taking me to the control room!"

"Don't worry, Captain Stiltonix,"

Heeeelp!

Robotix replied. "I'll take care of everything!"

In a **solar minute**, he had untangled me from the dirty clothes. Together, we headed toward the control room.

But as we walked through a pair of **automatic** doors, they closed suddenly. Robotix was trapped between them!

SOLAR-SMOKED GOUDA! What was going on?

Robotix managed to yank himself free and we continued walking. But the next set of *automatic* doors also closed suddenly — right on my tail. OUCH!

Next we came to a vertical sliding door. We pressed the red button to open it, but the door only raised a tiny bit. Robotix and I

Help!

swishhh

Ouch!

had no choice: We slithered under it like two **ASTROSLUGS** from planet Slothus.

When we saw the door to the control room, we B R E A T H E D a sigh of relief: We had finally arrived!

Oof!

Everything's Gone Haywire!

Inside the control room, it was complete **mayhem**. The equipment was making weird sounds, **SCREENS** were turning on and off on their own, and the crew looked more stressed than a bunch of elfix on the **Night of the Dancing Stars***!

No one even noticed me — well, except for my grandfather, the retired **Admiral William Stiltonix**.

"Grandson!" he thundered. "Where have you **been**? This is a disaster. None of the ship's equipment *works* anymore!"

"I, er . . ." I squeaked. "Well, the alarm

*Read all about the elfix in my book *Away in a Star Sled*!

17

clock went off late . . . um, my stylist gave me the wrong uniform —"

"ENOUGH WITH THE EXCUSES!" Grandfather interrupted me. "Get to your station and start behaving like a real captain!"

I hurried over to my captain's chair, walking right past my cousin Trap.

My uniform!

And that's my uniform!

"Hi, Cuz!" he shouted. "So that's where my **CLOTHES** went!"

I realized then that he was wearing **my** captain's uniform!

"What's going on?" I asked him, **pointing** to his clothes. "Trap, why are you wearing my clothes?"

"I don't have a clue!" he replied. "This morning my automatic **stylist** handed me this uniform. He said it was Hologramix's order. I thought it was a **JOKE**!"

Hologramix, our ship's super-high-tech computer, was usually very serious, and not big on **pranks**. I looked over at it—

and saw that its image was fuzzy and faded. **How weird!**

"Do you know what's happening?" I asked my sister, Thea. She has an **explanation** for just about everything.

"We're just not sure," Thea replied. "Hologramix started acting strangely this morning, and now **nothing** on the ship is working **PROPERLY**."

At that moment, **Sally de Wrench**, our ship's technical genius, entered the control room.

"I know what's wrong," she said.

Ooohhh!

"HOLOGRAMIX IS SICK!"

Is It a Virus?

Shooting stars! This was **SERIOUS**!

"The possibility that this would happen was ONE IN A TRILLION, but it happened!" Sally explained nervously.

"But how does a computer get **sick**?!" I asked, incredulous.

"The circuits are all fine, the memory is intact, and the processor has no damage," Sally explained. "But **something** isn't working like before! Hologramix looks too tired to perform the thousands of transactions it needs to complete each day. It looks like it might be some kind of virus."

"But you can **FIX** it, right?" I asked.

Sally shook her head. "Unfortunately I don't know how to **fix** it because I don't really know what's **wrong**," she said, a worried look on her snout.

Cosmic cheddar! Without Hologramix, the *MouseStar 1* was stuck!

Right then, my nephew Benjamin ran to me and gave me a huge hug.

"Hologramix will get **better**, right, Uncle G?" he asked sweetly.

HOLOGRAMIX
MouseStar 1's onboard computer

Species: Ultra-advanced artificial intelligence
Specialty: Controls all functions on the ship, including the autopilot function
Characteristics: Considers itself to be indispensable
Defining Features: Appears wherever and whenever it's needed

"Of course!" I said confidently, trying to reassure him. "Sally, there has to be **SOMETHING** we can do."

"I'm afraid the only one who can help Hologramix is Professor Twisterix," Sally replied. "He was my teacher at the *University for Lunar Physics and Galactic Engineering*. He taught me everything I know about engineering, and he helped me **design** Hologramix many galactic years ago!"

"Let's call him right away!" I squeaked excitedly.

"I'm afraid it's not that easy," Sally said, **SIGHING**. "The professor retired to spend time on his **INVENTIONS**. I think he might still live on planet Factorix near the university. But I don't know his address; he's **extremely** private!"

"Maybe we can find his phone number in the Intergalactic Phone Directory," I suggested.

Sally shook her head. "I tried looking him up last year," she said. "But his **NUMBER** isn't listed!"

"Well, we can't waste any time!" Grandfather William thundered. "What are you waiting for, Geronimo? If Hologramix shuts down completely, we're in supergalactic **trouble**!"

"Um . . . you're right, Grandfather," I replied.

"Of course I'm right!" he squeaked. "Start planning an expedition **IMMEDIATELY**!"

Have I mentioned that it's a terrible idea to contradict Grandfather William?

"Yes, Grandfather!" I replied quickly.

"Hooray!" Benjamin squeaked joyfully. "I've heard planet **FACTORIX** is home to the most mouserific inventions in the entire galaxy! I can come, too — can't I, Uncle?"

My little nephew looked up at me *sweetly*. He looked so excited, I couldn't say no.

"Of course you can," I reassured him.

And that was the beginning of our incredible intergalactic adventure!

A Galaxy of Trouble

Planning the expedition was especially difficult with **HOLOGRAMIX** out of order.

First of all, where in the name of cheddar was planet Factorix? Luckily, *MouseStar 1*'s **superstellar GPS navigator** seemed to be working. In a few seconds, it displayed our route.

Thea overrode the **automatic pilot** so she could fly the ship manually. It wouldn't have been a **GOOD IDEA** to use the autopilot when Hologramix wasn't working properly!

Thank goodmouse Thea is such a good pilot, because we quickly ended up in a **galaxy** of trouble. She had to steer the ship

through a thick meteor shower, a magnetic storm, and a cloud of stardust! Luckily, we made it through with **no damage**.

"Can someone tell me what's going on?!" Thea asked. "Why did the **SUPERSTELLAR GPS NAVIGATOR** send us this way? This route is too **dangerous**!"

Sally examined the device.

"You're right, Thea!" she replied. "I didn't realize the GPS navigator wouldn't be working correctly, but it makes sense. I forgot that Hologramix **controls** all the electronics on the ship!"

Stinky space cheese, what were we going to do now?

"Spacemice, forget about **TECHNOLOGY**," Grandfather William said. "Today we'll travel like we did in the olden days!"

From the Encyclopedia Galactica

SPACE NAVIGATION ATLAS

The space navigation atlas is an ancient navigational system used by spaceship captains before the invention of the computerized space navigator. The atlas has thousands of pages, including maps of the entire universe, listed in alphabetical order by galaxy. Once he or she locates the map of the star or planet, the captain must use his or her skills to navigate there.

Then he slammed down a dusty book on the table.

"Uh, as much as I LOVE to read, Grandfather, I'm not sure this is the best time . . ." I began.

"What are you talking about, Grandson?" he replied, a stern look on his snout. "This is a space navigation atlas! You'll need to use it to find Factorix."

Then he opened the book and began

looking for the map of the planet we were heading for.

"You know, when I was growing up, we didn't have **COMPUTERS**. Instead, I had to learn to read **SPACE MAPS**," he said. Then he exclaimed, "Ah, here's Factorix!"

"That's mouserific, Grandfather!" Thea replied. "You're the best!"

"Thank you, Thea!" he said, looking pleased with himself. "Now go back to the navigation controls. I just need a minute to consult the map. Then I'll help you figure out the best **route** through space."

A few moments later, we made a **RIGHT TURN** after the **PERSEUS** constellation, proceeded **STRAIGHT** to the crossroad between Galaxy 643 and Galaxy 981, and sped past the very bright star Maia. Finally, we saw the planet Factorix in front of us!

Even from far away I could tell it was a very **modern** planet covered in tall, high-tech buildings.

"Thea, Sally, Trap, Benjamin: Prepare for landing!" I ordered. "I'll meet you in the Teletransportix room!"

Sally cleared her throat.

"Um, I don't think the Teletransportix is

From the Encyclopedia Galactica

PLANET FACTORIX

This extremely modern planet is the location of the University for Lunar Physics and Galactic Engineering. Aliens from galaxies all over the universe study and live here peacefully together.

the best **way to go** right now, Captain!" she squeaked helpfully.

Superstellar Swiss! She was right. How **CARELESS** of me! With Hologramix out of order, we couldn't risk using the **Teletransportix**. I didn't want to end up on Factorix while my tail was left behind on the *MouseStar 1*. I'm too fond of my fur for that!

"Thanks, Sally," I replied. "We'll use a **space pod** instead. See you at the launch dock!"

Sally was the last one to get to the pod. She had disconnected Hologramix and placed the computer in a *special* container full of protective Parmesan cheese slices that had been prepared by our ship's onboard **scientist**, Professor Greenfur.

"Captain, with Hologramix out of order, I had to set *MouseStar 1* on **standby mode**," Sally told me.

"**STANDBY** what?" I squeaked.

"It's as if our **SPACESHIP** has been turned off," Sally explained. "Only the lighting, air, and water systems are still running."

SHOOTING STARS! This was **serious**. The *MouseStar 1* had never been turned **off** before.

"Quick! Let's get moving!" I told my crew. "We can't **WASTE** any time — we have to **CURE** Hologramix!"

WELCOME TO FACTORIX!

After traveling for another galactic hour, Thea steered the space pod into Factorix's very crowded spaceship port.

Galactic Gorgonzola, there were so many spaceships!

"A lot of **aliens** visit Factorix every day," Sally explained. "There are scientists, students on exchange programs, and aliens looking to purchase the **latest** and **GREATEST** inventions."

"**It's not going to be easy to find parking**," Thea muttered.

"There's a spot!" Trap squeaked.

My sister started pulling into the spot, when . . .

BEEEEEEEEEEEEEEEP!

An alien driving a sporty spaceship zoomed right past us, missing us by a whisker.

"Holey craters, what terrible manners!" Thea squeaked as she performed a series of complicated maneuvers. An astrosecond later, our space pod was parallel parked perfectly!

Watch out!

"Here we are!" Thea announced as she turned off the engine. "I think it's best if I stay here with the ship. Let's stay in touch with our **WRIST PHONES**. Good luck scouting around!"

"Sounds good!" I said. Then I turned to Sally. "Um . . . where are we going?"

"To the UNIVERSITY, of course!" she replied. "If I recall correctly, it should be that way!"

She pointed to the left and we started walking. Luckily, we found some SIGNS that confirmed Sally had been right. In no time, we reached an enormouse, elegant, modern building.

From the Encyclopedia Galactica

UNIVERSITY FOR LUNAR PHYSICS AND GALACTIC ENGINEERING

This is the biggest university in the Cheddar Galaxy, and the home of the most prestigious inventions in the universe. Each year, millions of aliens from all around the galaxy come to the university to study, develop new inventions, and sharpen their intellect in the hopes of becoming universally known stellar scientists.

"Here we are!" Sally squeaked.

"**WOW!**" Benjamin exclaimed as he looked around him, awestruck. "Uncle G, when I'm old enough, do you think I can **study** here? I want to become the most mouserific inventor in the whole universe!"

I looked at my nephew **proudly**.

"If you work hard in school now, **I'm sure you can, Benjamin**!" I replied.

"Wait until you see what's inside," Sally told us. "It's even more **interesting**!"

"Well, what are we waiting for?" Trap asked. **"LET'S GO!"**

Wait until you see it!

Let's go!

Wow!

LET ME DOWN, PLEASE!

The **hallways** were crowded with aliens from all over the Cheddar Galaxy. They were moving quickly **IN** and **OUT** of classrooms and labs.

"Oh, how I love this place!" Sally said warmly as she looked around. "Let's go to the main office. Maybe someone there can tell us where we can find **PROFESSOR TWISTERIX**."

As we headed down one hallway after another, I sneaked a peek inside one of the **LABS**. A group of aliens was in the middle of an experiment when . . .

PUUUUUFFF!

A cloud of dust surrounded me, clinging to my clothes. Suddenly, I was **FLYING** through the air!

"Sorry!" a student said apologetically. "Our **antigravitational spray uniform** is still a prototype."

"Uh, no problem," I replied, trying to remain **CALM**. "But can you let me **down**, please?!"

In the meantime, Trap took off down the hallway in a pair of very **strange** shoes. A student ran after him, shouting.

"Sir, I told you not to **TOUCH** those!" he squeaked. "They're **rocket shoes**, but we're still testing them!"

As if that wasn't enough, a mail robot had **accidentally** picked up Benjamin and was delivering him to one of the classrooms like a package!

Two students stopped the mail robot immediately.

"Our flying mail robot is a work in progress," one explained sheepishly.

I ran over to my sweet nephew to make sure he was okay.

"Uncle Ger, you should have seen the eco-friendly engine on that robot!" Benjamin squeaked excitedly. "It runs on slime from the planet Slimix!"

"I'm glad you're okay," I told him, smiling. "Now we have to get to the office."

When we finally got there, a robot was assisting a long line of students. Finally, it was our turn.

"Hello," Sally said. "We would like to talk to Professor Twisterix. Can you schedule an appointment right away? It's urgent."

"Professor Arthur Twisterix retired three

galactic years ago," the robot replied mechanically.

"But do you know where we can find him now?" Sally asked, a **worried** look on her snout. "It's very **important**."

"I do not have access to the professor's current address," the robot replied.

And with that, he moved on to the **ALIEN** behind us in the line.

Mousey meteors! We were right back where we had started!

Next alien, please!

FOLLOW THAT SCENT

"What do we do now?" Sally asked, disappointed.

Suddenly, we heard a **soft** squeak behind us. "Excuse me, I accidentally overheard that you are looking for Professor Twisterix."

We turned to see an alien holding two br**ooms**, a **dustpan**, a **bucket**, and a **MOP** in her many tentacle-like arms.

"Yes!" I said eagerly. "Can you help us?"

"I think so," she replied. "I'm **AMELIA SHINIX**, the university's head cleaning alien. I've been working here for a thousand galactic years, so I know **EVERYTHING** about **everybody**. I think I know where you can find the **PROFESSOR**."

"That's **WONDERFUL**!" Sally exclaimed

happily. "Would you be so **kind** as to tell us?"

Amelia Shinix took a step closer.

I'm Amelia Shinix!

"He was recently seen in **Inventor's Alley**," she whispered. "That's a neighborhood on the other side of town. I hear he's starting his own **secret** laboratory."

"Thank you, Amelia!" Sally replied. "You've been so **helpful**."

We followed her directions and headed straight across town to **Inventor's Alley**. There we found a real **maze** of labs and workshops. Everywhere we looked there were aliens building and fixing all different kinds of **MECHANICAL EQUIPMENT**. We asked for the professor, but no one had **HEARD** of him!

"Hmm. How about we stop for a snack?" Trap said. "I can smell **cheesy Pluto peas**!"

"Hold on a second!" Sally exclaimed. "Cheesy Pluto peas are the professor's favorite **dish**! Perhaps we'll find him if we follow the **SCENT**."

Holey craters, what a mouserific idea!

Trap started sniffing and we followed. He led us to a **bizarre-looking** building made completely of spare parts.

"This is where the SMELL is coming from," Trap declared. "Oh, I'm so **hungry**!"

Sally knocked on the door. A second later, it opened, and we were **snout-to-snout** with an older rodent.

"Stellar circuits! It's Sally de Wrench, my smartest student!" he exclaimed. "**What a shocking surprise!**"

"Professor Twisterix!" Sally squeaked happily. "How nice to see you again!"

Mmm . . . the smell of cheesy Pluto peas!

Sally hugged the professor. He was a friendly-looking alien with **green** skin, **REDDISH** hair, and **E I G H T** arms.

"And who are your friends?" he asked.

"I'm Geronimo Stiltonix," I said, extending a paw. "I'm the captain of the spaceship *MouseStar 1*. This is my cousin Trap and my nephew Benjamin."

Professor Twisterix invited us into his **HOME LABORATORY**. Martian mozzarella, I had never seen a more **DISGUSTING** place!

"Pardon the **MESS**, but I've been working on a new prototype," the professor said.

Trap looked at the pot of **cheesy Pluto peas** the professor was holding.

"Well, actually, I was just taking a break for a little snack," Professor Twisterix explained. "Would you like to join me?"

Everyone declined politely except **TRAP**. He grabbed a spoon and happily dug in.

"Thank you, Professor!" my cousin exclaimed happily.

Slurp!

"It's a real pleasure to meet another true gourmet!"

I HAVE EXACTLY
WHAT YOU NEED!

"**Stellar circuits, how did you find me?**" our host asked once he and Trap had finished their snack.

"It was thanks to Amelia Shinix!" Sally replied. "But why all this **SECRECY**?"

"I wanted to completely dedicate myself to my inventions, with no distractions," the professor explained. "Would you like to take a look at my latest work?"

"We would love to, but first we need to ask for your help!" Sally explained.

The professor **looked concerned**.

"Do you remember Hologramix, the computer I created for my thesis project?" Sally went on.

"**BUT OF COURSE!**" the professor replied. "I helped you design that hologram with a mouse's snout."

"Exactly!" Sally squeaked. "Unfortunately, Hologramix isn't working properly. I don't know what the **problem** is!"

"Hmmm . . . interesting," the professor said. "Let me take a look."

Sally GENTLY placed the box on the table and turned Hologramix on: Its snout was as faded and tired-looking as ever.

Professor **Twisterix** examined it, mumbling to himself as he worked.

"It could be a side short **circuit** . . . or maybe there's been some damage to the quantum chip . . ."

I don't know much about **machines** and I didn't want to get in the **way**, so I sat away from the others, on a **COMFY** chair made of old mechanical parts.

I was just about to drift off to **SLEEP** when something bumped against my paw. I jumped up, screaming.

"**AHHHH!**" I yelped. "What was that?"

Trap just laughed.

"Ha, ha, ha!" he chuckled. "You're such a scaredy-mouse, Cuz! *It's just a sweet robot doggy.*"

I glanced down at the little creature and was about to reply when the professor's voice interrupted my thoughts.

"**I've got it!**" he cried. "It's the power generator! Your onboard computer is *running out of juice*!"

"Ah, that explains why the reboot process was so slow . . ." Sally mused.

"**Um, does that mean Hologramix isn't really broken?**" I asked hopefully. "And there's no virus?"

"Correct!" the professor replied. "It's only out of **power**. All you need is a new **battery** from planet Energix. I should have one around here somewhere . . ."

He began searching through **parts**, **tools**, and other **JUNK** around the lab.

"Not here . . . not there . . . nope . . . oh, I think I know where it is!" he muttered. Then he walked straight to a closet in the back of the **LAB**, opened its door and . . .

Crash!

"Professor, are you **okay**?" Sally asked.

After a moment of silence, he came up *shaking* his snout.

"Unfortunately the battery isn't here," he said **seriously**. "And it was the last one in the whole **universe**: The energy on planet Energix has completely **RUN OUT**!"

"B-but there must b-be **SOMETHING** we can do!" I stuttered anxiously.

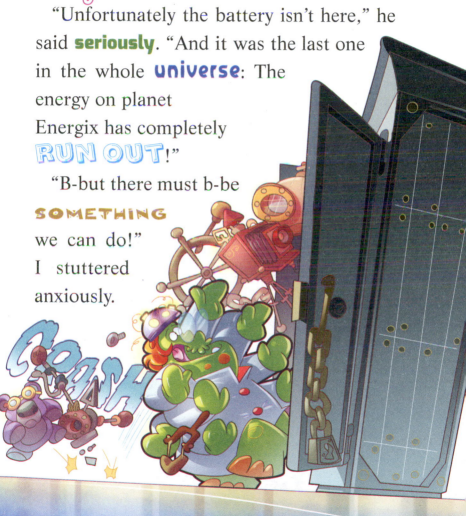

Professor Twisterix shook his head **SADLY**. "In the past, we thought the **POWER** on Energix was inexhaustible, but we were wrong."

Sally sighed. Everyone else in the lab was very, very quiet.

"Stellar circuits, why didn't I think of it before?!" Professor Twisterix exclaimed suddenly. Then he grabbed a tool and began to **explain**. "This is an energy transformer. It can convert **galactic wind** and **STARLIGHT** into **electrical energy**. It's only a prototype, but it should work fine with Hologramix's specifications!"

I've got it!

"That's great news!" I squeaked happily.

"Do you mean Hologramix can be fixed, and it will also be more **ecologically friendly**?" Benjamin asked.

Twisterix smiled.

"That's right, young mouse," he replied. "I'll get right to **work**. Come back tomorrow at the same time and I should be done."

Then the professor lowered his voice and looked around NERVOUSLY. "Please keep this to yourselves!" he urged us. "This is brand-new technology, and there are always aliens trying to steal SECRETS around here!"

Then he called the ROBOT DOG over to him.

"Fidox, please take them to their space pod!"

Time to Celebrate!

We happily followed the professor's robot dog through the neighborhood's very crowded streets.

"What a **successful** mission!" Trap squeaked excitedly. "Thanks to Twisterix's **clever** invention, we won't have any more problems with Hologramix!"

I noticed that some of the aliens around us glanced our way. Why does my cousin always have to be so **BOISTEROUS** and **LOUD**?

"Trap, would you please lower your voice?" I implored him. "Remember what the professor said!"

But he wasn't listening.

"Turning stellar wind into energy is

a brilliant idea!" Trap practically shouted.

A few aliens moved even closer to us, perking up their ears. *Holey craters*, I had to think of something to get my cousin to stop **squeaking**!

"Trap, please —" I tried to say, but before I could even finish the sentence, a big alien

Hey, how rude!

in a **BLACK CAPE** bumped into me, almost knocking me down.

"How rude!" I squeaked, but he had already disappeared into the crowd. The air around him smelled of **moldy sardines**! Ugh!

"Quiet, Trap!" Sally exclaimed. "The professor asked us to keep a **secret**, and there may be NOSY aliens around us."

Trap finally stopped talking, and we made our way back to Thea and our spacecraft.

After we said good-bye to FIDOX, we flew back to the *MouseStar 1* for the night.

CLUMSY, RUDE ALIENS!

The following day, we headed straight back to the secret lab. Once again, Thea waited for us at the **spaceship port**, while Trap, Sally, Benjamin, and I went to meet Professor Twisterix.

As before, the streets of Inventor's Alley were crowded with all kinds of **ALIENS** busily buying, selling, and fixing the **weirdest** objects.

"I can't wait to see Hologramix again!" I squeaked. I would be so relieved once Hologramix was healthy and back on board the *MouseStar 1*.

"Me too, because . . . **ouch**!" Trap said. A huge alien in a big black cape had just

How rude!

CRASHED into him.

Martian mozzarella! It was the alien who had bumped into me the previous day! I recognized the same **STINKY STENCH** of moldy sardines!

I was about to say something when two smaller aliens **BUMPED** into me, knocking me down. Ouch!

"What clumsy, rude aliens!" Trap mumbled.

"Everything okay, **Captain**?" Sally asked as she helped me up.

"Yes, but I know I've seen those two aliens *somewhere* before," I said. I just couldn't recall where.

We finally arrived at Twisterix's workshop. Sally knocked on the door.

There was no answer.

We waited a minute and then tried again.

Again, there was no answer.

"Professor!" Trap shouted loudly as we knocked a third time.

Once again, there was no answer.

"That's strange," Sally said quietly. "Professor Twisterix may be secretive, but he's always **VERY METICULOUS** and **PUNCTUAL**!"

"Maybe he went out for a bit," I suggested.

"I hope he's okay," Sally went on, a **worried** look on her snout.

"We'll just have to find out!" Trap said as he approached the outside wall of the building and stood on the TIPS of his paws, peeking in a window.

Hmmm . . .

What do you see?

"Can you see anything?" Benjamin asked. Trap took another look.

"There's no sign of the professor, but there's a **box** with a note on it sitting on the table," Trap told us.

"**Can you read the note?**" I asked eagerly.

"Yes," he replied. "It says: **FOR THE SPACEMICE!**"

Mousey meteorites! Why was there a box for us in the lab but no sign of Professor Twisterix?

This mission had suddenly taken a strange turn!

THERE'S SOMETHING FISHY GOING ON

It was very suspicious that Twisterix wasn't home at the **T**i**ME** we had agreed on. And it was even more suspicious that there was a box for us in his lab instead of him!

We decided to go **inside** to see if we could find any **clues** to explain what was going on. Sally got out her special **multipurpose tool** and used it to unlock the door. It has a sensor that can open and close all kinds of locks!

Sally put the tool in the **LOCK**, and the door to the lab opened.

"What a great **INVENTION**!" I squeaked.

"Thank you, Captain!" Sally replied. "I was able to design it because I studied with Professor Twisterix."

As soon as we got inside, we took a look at the box on the table. It **LOOKED** like the box Hologramix had been packed in.

"Perhaps the professor had an emergency and left **HOLOGRAMIX** all fixed up for us," Trap thought out loud.

"Hmm . . . that's not like him," Sally squeaked. "And he would have left a note on the **DOOR**, not in the lab."

"There's only one way we can **FIND OUT** if Hologramix is here: We have to turn the box on!"

So Sally pushed a **button**. A bright **beam of light** shined out of the box. But instead of Hologramix's snout, it was the hologram of a **BABY BiRD**!

70

"And **who** are you?" Sally asked, taken aback.

The hologram replied **mechanically**: "Can a cat play patty-cake? *Paw*-sibly! Ha, ha, ha!"

Martian mozzarella!

Was it telling jokes?

We were all quiet while the **BaBY BiRD** hologram went on: "What did the zero say to the eight? Nice belt! Ha, ha, ha!"

Can a cat play patty-cake?

We **looked** at one another, dumbfounded. Then we all burst out laughing.

"Do you like my **JOKES**?"

the baby bird asked. "Here's another one: Why do mice need oiling? Because they squeak!"

Black holey galaxies! Why had Professor Twisterix left a weird, robotic **BABY BIRD** hologram for us?

"Let me check something out," Sally said. Then she pushed some **BUTTONS** to turn off the box and unlocked a little compartment

on the bottom with her **multipurpose tool**. "It's just as I thought. This isn't Hologramix, but a toy for the alien mouselets of **planet Gigglyx**!" Sally declared.

"B-but what kind of a **JOKE** is this?" I asked.

Sally looked puzzled as well. "There's definitely something **fishy** going on here," she said.

Suddenly, Trap shushed us.

"Quiet!" he whispered. "**CAN YOU HEAR THAT?**"

We pricked up our ears and heard a very soft

"It sounds like it's coming from the closet over there," Benjamin squeaked. "**LET'S GO SEE!**"

We opened the doors of the closet and found Professor Twisterix inside! He had been **bound** and **GAGGED**!

TO CATCH A THIEF!

We quickly untied the professor, and he filled us in on what had happened.

"About two GaLactic hours ago, three aliens suddenly burst into the lab," he explained. "Two of them bound and GAGGED me and locked me in the closet. In the meantime, I heard the other one remove Hologramix, which I had just FIXED. Meanwhile, the other two chattered about leaving a 'little gift' for you spacemice."

"Did you get a good look at the aliens?" I asked him.

Twisterix shook his head.

"Stellar Swiss, not really!" he said. "Everything happened so quickly, and then they locked me in the closet."

"I'm so sorry, Professor!" Sally said sadly. "I feel responsible. I didn't mean to get you into **TROUBLE**!"

"It's not your fault," Professor Twisterix reassured her. "Those three came with the intention of stealing **HOLOGRAMIX**, not hurting me! But how did they know it was here? Did you talk to anybody?"

"**ABSOLUTELY NOT!**" I squeaked. But then I remembered how loudly Trap had been talking in the street the previous day. **Martian mozzarella!** Someone had overheard him!

Trap seemed to have the same thought.

"I'm so sorry," he admitted, hanging his snout. "I made a *mistake* yesterday. I was so **HAPPY** we had accomplished our mission that I spoke a little too **LOUDLY** while we were walking down the street."

"There are open eyes and ears everywhere on this planet," Twisterix replied, shaking his head. "I warned you to be careful."

I sighed, leaning my paw on the table.

OUCH!

A sharp, protruding nail stuck my fur. As I massaged my hurt paw, I noticed a scrap of **BLACK CLOTH** had caught on the nail. **Where had I seen that fabric before?**

Holey craters, of course! It looked just like the **black cape** the alien who had **bumped** into me and Trap in the street had been wearing! He must be the thief!

I explained my **THEORY** to the others.

"At least we know who to look for now," I said. "Spacemice, let's go!"

"Please, let me help!" Professor Twisterix said. Then he whistled for the cute **robot dog** we had met the previous day.

"If the thieves are still on planet Factorix, they won't be able to **get away** from this guy!" he explained. "Fidox has the most **AMAZING** mechanical sense of smell in the entire universe. He can recognize and analyze **SEVEN BILLION** different scents!"

"Wow!" Benjamin squeaked in awe.

The professor grabbed the piece of black cloth and placed it under the dog's nose. Fidox began **BARKING** immediately.

Woof! Woof!

Then he headed for the door.

"Follow him!" Twisterix urged us. "He's equipped with a high-tech **intergalactic tracking device**. I'll monitor your movements from here. If you should need help, I'll know **EXACTLY** where you are!"

PIRATE SPACECAT ALERT!

We **RACED** through the streets of Factorix on Fidox's heels. Martian mozzarella, that robot dog moved **FAST**!

"That dog is . . . **huff** . . . quick!" I squeaked between breaths.

"Why aren't there astrotaxis on this planet?" Trap moaned in reply.

"I think Fidox is heading toward the SPACESHIP PORT," Sally said.

"COME ON!" Benjamin urged us. "We're almost there!"

"I . . . *puff* . . . hope so!" I replied. "I don't

Come on!

He's leading us to the spaceship port!

think I can make it much *farther*!"

Thankfully, my sweet nephew was right: The ROBOT DOG stopped running as soon as we reached the spaceship port. He barked once and then carefully led us through the parked ships. He stopped in front of one with a black flag with a fish bone on it.

Mousey meteors! That flag was the symbol of the PIRATE SPACECATS*! They are feared across the galaxy. They love to invade planets and steal whatever precious treasures they find. Just thinking about their ruthless captain, Black Star, made my fur stand on end! Were the pirate spacecats the thieves?

"Quick, hide!" Sally WHISPERED, pointing to the spaceship. "Someone's coming!"

*We spacemice met the pirate spacecats in *The Underwater Planet*.

We quickly slipped around a corner. From there we **peered** out and saw three pirate spacecats exit the spaceship.

"Thanks to this **onboard computer** and this tool that provides endless power, we'll be the most feared creatures in the entire galaxy!" one of them exclaimed.

Shh! Quiet, fishbrains!

"Argh!" another one cackled. "But aren't we the most feared **already**?"

"Well, yes," the first spacecat replied. "But now we'll be even scarier! We came to this planet for a small engine **repair** and look what we got instead? **Bwa, ha, ha, ha, ha!**"

Suddenly, **Black Star** emerged from the space ship and joined the other three. His **twirly** black whiskers looked as evil as ever. And I noticed that his black cape had a **TEAR** in the back! There was no doubt about it: He had stolen **HOLOGRAMIX**!

"Quiet, fishbrains!" he barked, hushing his crew. "Galaxia, have you checked out the new onboard computer as I ordered?"

"Sure, Captain!" one of the spacecats replied. "It works **PERFECTLY**!"

"Excellent!" Black Star growled. "Now go

get me something to eat! **Moldy sardines** would be ideal."

"Right on, Captain!" came the reply.

"**Hurry up!**" the mean pirate replied. "I want to leave this flea-ridden planet before nightfall."

Moldy sardines . . . yummy!

The three pirate spacecats **took off** immediately, disappearing into the city streets.

Left on his own, **Black Star** extended his claws and began sharpening them on a stone.

Squeak!

HOW SCARY!

86

HERE'S THE PLAN . . .

"Did you hear that?" Sally whispered. "The pirate spacecats have already *set up* Hologramix as their spaceship's onboard computer. We have to get Hologramix back before their ship leaves or we might **NEVER** find them again!"

"I've got this!" Trap squeaked confidently. "I took three cosmic karate classes last year—"

"Wait!" I cried. "Don't do anything *foolish*, Trap! Did you see **Black Star**'s claws? And

I'll take care of it!

did you hear those other feline meanies? They are the **scariest** creatures in the galaxy! If one of those cats catches us, we'll be *minced spacemice*!"

"Geronimo is right," Sally agreed. "We need to come up with a plan to get into their spaceship and rescue Hologramix before those rascals get back!"

We were all quiet as we tried to come up with an **IDEA**. Even Fidox seemed to be thinking as he **nuzzled** his robotic snout against my paw. As I patted his head, an idea came to me **SUDDENLY**.

"Martian mozzarella!" I exclaimed. "I've got it: Let's have Fidox distract Black Star while we slip into the spaceship and take back **HOLOGRAMIX**!"

Trap seemed doubtful, but Sally's eyes lit up.

"That's a simply brilliant plan, Captain!" she squeaked.

My fur turned as **RED** as the planet Mars. Oh, how embarrassing! I can't help blushing whenever Sally pays me a **COMPLIMENT**.

But my sweet nephew looked worried.

"What is it?" I asked, concerned.

"What if Black Star **grabs** Fidox and tries to steal or hurt him?" he asked.

"Don't worry," I assured him. "You saw how quickly that robot can *run*, right? And he clearly knows this planet like the back of his mechanical paw. **Even if Black Star wanted to, he could never catch Fidox!"**

Woof! Woof!

Benjamin smiled, and the robot dog barked and wagged his tail happily, as if to prove my point.

"Go on, then, Fidox," Benjamin said, patting the robot dog's head. "Our fate is in your paws!"

The little robot dog ran straight toward the **SPACESHIP**. Then he started barking to get Black Star's attention. As soon as the evil pirate captain glanced over at Fidox, the dog jumped up and began scratching the SHINY hull of the spaceship with his metal paws.

"Hey, what are you doing, you MECHANICAL MUTT?" Black Star shouted. "Go away!"

Fidox kept his paws on the hull.

"Oh yeah?" the pirate GROWLED. "Get your greasy robot paws off my spaceship right now! Or I'll have fun taking you apart P I E C E by P I E C E! You'll be a pile of scrap metal in no time."

Black Star *lunged* at Fidox, and the robotic pup took off, zipping in and out of the parked **SPACESHIPS**. Black Star followed him, growling and shaking his sharp claws at him.

Holey craters! Our plan had worked. Now it was our turn to slip onto the pirate's spaceship and rescue Hologramix!

"Trap, you stay on guard duty," I said. "If any of the **pirate spacecats** come back, whistle loudly. Sally and Benjamin, follow me! It's time to FREE Hologramix!"

TRAPPED!

The inside of the spaceship was so **dark** we had to use our wrist phone **flashlights** to see. Sally quickly figured out the way to the control room, and we followed her, **single file**.

Suddenly, a door opened and we **heard** Hologramix!

"Who are you?" its voice demanded as a huge hologram in the shape of a spacecat's face materialized in front of us.

Martian mozzarella, what was going on?

The hologram **LOOKED** like a spacecat, but it sounded just like Hologramix!

"Wh-what?!" I stuttered. "Who are **WE**? Who are **YOU**?"

"Who am I?!" the hologram replied. "I am Holocattix, this spaceship's onboard computer. And you cheesebrains are all **trespassing**!"

"No, you're Hologramix," Sally squeaked. "You're *MouseStar 1*'s onboard computer!"

"**Ha, Ha, Ha!**" Holocattix cackled. "That's funny! You're on the wrong spaceship. What are you doing here, you **rascally rodents**?"

I tried to squeak, but my throat was so dry, **nothing** came out.

"The pirate spacecats stole you and reconfigured you," Sally tried to explain. "You really belong to the spacemice. We're here to **RESCUE** you and take you back to the *MouseStar 1* with us!"

But it was impossible to reason with Holocattix.

"The pirate spacecats aren't thieves!" the hologram replied. "I think you **rats** are the thieves, and this is what we do to **THIEVES** around here . . ."

Suddenly, two scary **flying robots** stormed in through an opening in the ceiling. They looked like giant **SPACE INSECTS**. They buzzed above us menacingly

as the door to the command room closed behind us.

WE WERE TRAPPED!

"Now we'll wait for Black Star," the hologram growled. "He'll decide what to do with you! Ha, ha, ha!"

I tried to contact Trap with my wrist phone, but as soon as I touched it . . .

My wrist phone turned off, as if the battery had died.

Holocattix laughed.

"Did you really think I would let you use your communication device?" it cackled. "Wishful thinking, rascally rodent! HA, HA, HA!"

TELL US A STORY, CAPTAIN!

Stinky space cheese! What were we going to do? As long as Hologramix continued to believe it was really a pirate spacecat, we were in **big trouble**! It seemed we had no choice but to wait for **Black Star** to return.

As we waited, I stared at Hologramix — I mean, **Holocattix**. I recalled my first days as captain of the *MouseStar 1*. Back then, I had **no clue** how to operate a spaceship. Thankfully, Hologramix had been there to **HELP ME**. I don't know what I would have done otherwise!

With nothing else to do as we waited, I began reminiscing fondly about those days.

"Hologramix was the best onboard

computer a captain could ever wish for," I said with a sigh. "On my first mission to **URANUS**, I forgot all the equipment, even my thermal **undershirt**! But Hologramix realized it before I did and sent a **shuttle** with all the necessities."

Benjamin listened eagerly, a **SWEET** smile on his snout.

"Go on," he said encouragingly. "Tell us another story, Uncle!"

"Well, I also remember when we hosted the president of the **INTERSTELLAR FREEDOM FEDERATION** on the *MouseStar 1*. At the gala *reception*, I brought my grocery list up to the podium instead of my welcome speech! But Hologramix saved the day by mimicking my voice and **RECITING** the speech for me. It was truly fabumouse how Hologramix **saved my snout**!"

"Keep going, Captain!" Sally whispered. "I think something's happening to Holocattix!"

I looked up to see *static* breaking up the hologram of the pirate spacecat's face. GREAT GALAXIES! It seemed like Holocattix was turning back into Hologramix again!

"Your stories seem to be triggering some of Hologramix's MEMORIES," Sally explained. "Those emotions are helping to remind Hologramix who it really is."

So I began to **recount** one more incident. "One time, I thought I had lost my very precious notebook, when —"

"I activated **MouseStar 1**'s control sensors," a familiar voice cut in. It was Hologramix! "I was able to find your notebook just before it was shredded by the ship's **superstellar paper recycling machine**!"

I looked up to see a digital mouse snout *smiling* at me.

"Look!" Benjamin squeaked excitedly. "The hologram changed!"

Stinky space cheese! Hologramix was back!

Aye Aye, Captain Stiltonix!

"**CAPTAIN!** What are you doing here?" Hologramix exclaimed. "Actually, what am **I** doing here? This is not the *MouseStar 1*!"

"It's a long story," Sally began. "Basically, you were mousenapped and **re-configured** by Black Star and his pirate spacecats."

"But how?" Hologramix asked. "Also when, where, and why?!"

"We don't have time to explain it all now," I said quickly. "We have to **GET OUT** of here before the pirate spacecats return. Please turn off these two **INSECT ROBOTS** and turn on our wrist phones?"

"**Aye aye, Captain Stiltonix!**" Hologramix

replied.

As soon as my wrist phone was working, I called Trap.

"**Mission accomplished!**" I announced. "We have **HOLOGRAMIX** back and we're leaving the pirate spacecats' ship. We'll meet you back at our spaceship!"

"Just a sec, Captain," Trap replied. "**I have a special delivery for the pirates!**"

So as Sally, Benjamin, Hologramix, and I dashed out of Black Star's ship, Trap slipped past us. He was holding a strange-looking **little box** in his paws. Shortly afterward, he met us back at our spacecraft.

"What did you do?" I asked him, **curious**.

He grinned. "Nothing, really," he replied. "I just left a little surprise for our **spacecat** 'friends' . . ."

A minute later, our shuttle was blasting

off into space as we headed back to the *MouseStar 1*. I glanced out the window to see Black Star running back to his spaceship, **gasping for air**.

Fidox had done a **mouserific** job tiring him out!

I got out my space telescope and **watched** through the window as Black Star boarded his ship. I saw him pick up the package Trap had left for him. Then he began **shaking** his paw angrily and **SHOUTING** something. He must have

Huff! Puff!

realized we had taken back Hologramix!

Soon Black Star was sitting at his spaceship's controls, **FIRING UP** the engines!

"Uh, Thea," I said *quickly*. "We have a problem! It looks like Black Star is coming after us!"

Trap just **chuckled**.

"No worries, Cuz," he said confidently, kicking up his paws. "He's not going anywhere."

Then he pulled a **REMOTE CONTROL** from his pocket and pressed a button. A moment later . . .

KA-BOOOOM!

Black Star's ship suddenly transformed into an amusement park, full of superstellar attractions like **floating slides**, **spinning satellites**, and **BUMPER SPACESHIPS**.

"B-but how did you do that?" I stuttered in shock.

"It's called a **portable intergalactic amusement park**!" Trap squeaked proudly. "It's a new space invention. When we were at the university, a group of **scientists** gave it to me as a sample. I figured this was a pretty good chance to use it!"

I glanced back out the window at the spaceship port as we flew away and saw a group of small **ALIENS** lining up to check out the new amusement park.

"Well done, Cuz!" I exclaimed. "Twisterix will be proud of you!"

HOLEY CRATERS! That reminded me that in the rush to **save** Hologramix and escape from the pirate spacecats, we had forgotten to say **good-bye** to the professor! But I was sure we would see him again someday . . .

EVERYTHING'S OKAY, GRANDFATHER!

When we got back to the *MouseStar 1*, it was very quiet. **Grandfather William** was the first to greet us. He **hugged** me tightly when he saw we had brought back Hologramix.

Galactic gorgonzola, I was **SHOCKED**! My grandfather isn't very **CUDDLY**, and he's definitely **not** usually a hugger! He must have been

mousetastically happy that our mission had succeeded.

As soon as Grandfather let me go, Sally and I got to work.

"Sally, let's plug in Hologramix **right away**!" I said excitedly.

"Of course, Captain!" she said as she got to work *immediately*. In just a few minutes, the doors on the *MouseStar 1* were opening and closing with no problems, the **LIFTRIX** was working efficiently, and the lights were back on. The only thing missing was the yellow snout of our **onboard computer**!

Suddenly, there was a shout behind me.

"Boo!" a voice squeaked.

Martian mozzarella! Who was it?

I turned around and . . . there was **HOLOGRAMIX**!

"Did you miss me, Captain?" it asked.

Before I could reply, a message appeared on the main screen: **Incoming Call!**

"Hologramix, take the call!" I insisted.

A second later, *Professor Twisterix* and Fidox appeared on the screen.

"Professor, how nice to see you again!" I greeted him.

"SUPERSTELLAR CIRCUITS!" the professor said. "I see you're all back SAFE and sound, including Hologramix! Congratulations on accomplishing your mission."

"It's all thanks to you and Fidox!" Sally replied.

"I was happy to help!" Professor Twisterix replied. "I see that your onboard computer is working, thanks to the power transformer. I'll send you the instructions so you can set up the *MouseStar 1*'s engines to run on the same system. Then you can use WIND and STARLIGHT energy to power your spaceship, too!"

"Do you mean we won't have to use TETRASTELLIUM to power our engines anymore?"

"That's right!" the professor confirmed.

"As soon as I set up the engines, we'll be able to *fly* using just the energy from the wind and stars!" Sally chimed in.

"Yay!" Benjamin cheered. "*MouseStar 1* will be the **most environmentally friendly spaceship in the Cheddar Galaxy**!"

"I have another idea," Professor Greenfur added. "If you agree, Professor Twisterix, Sally and I can fine-tune your invention to make it available to every spaceship in the universe!"

"What a mouserific idea!" Twisterix replied. "You have my permission to proceed!"

"Let's celebrate," Hologramix said as a robot waiter approached me holding a beverage. "This is for you, Captain. Cheers!"

I was about to take a sip when I realized

it was **MOTOR OIL**. Black holey galaxies! I looked at Hologramix in alarm, but he just winked.

"**Gotcha!**" he said, laughing.

Trap, Benjamin, Thea, Sally, Professor Greenfur, and I all **joined in**. It felt great to laugh after our **encounter** with the pirate spacecats. I had a feeling we hadn't seen the last of those famousely *ferocious* felines! But that, dear rodent friends, is a **story** for another day!

Don't miss any adventures of the Spacemice!

#1 Alien Escape

#2 You're Mine, Captain!

#3 Ice Planet Adventure

#4 The Galactic Goal

#5 Rescue Rebellion

#6 The Underwater Planet

#7 Beware! Space Junk!

#8 Away in a Star Sled

#9 Slurp Monster Showdown

#10 Pirate Spacecat Attack

Up Next!

#11 We'll Bite Your Tail, Geronimo!

Be sure to read all my fabumouse adventures!

#1 Lost Treasure of the Emerald Eye

#2 The Curse of the Cheese Pyramid

#3 Cat and Mouse in a Haunted House

#4 I'm Too Fond of My Fur!

#5 Four Mice Deep in the Jungle

#6 Paws Off, Cheddarface!

#7 Red Pizzas for a Blue Count

#8 Attack of the Bandit Cats

#9 A Fabumouse Vacation for Geronimo

#10 All Because of a Cup of Coffee

#11 It's Halloween, You 'Fraidy Mouse!

#12 Merry Christmas, Geronimo!

#13 The Phantom of the Subway

#14 The Temple of the Ruby of Fire

#15 The Mona Mousa Code

#16 A Cheese-Colored Camper

#17 Watch Your Whiskers, Stilton!

#18 Shipwreck on the Pirate Islands

#19 My Name Is Stilton, Geronimo Stilton

#20 Surf's Up, Geronimo!

#21 The Wild, Wild West

#22 The Secret of Cacklefur Castle

A Christmas Tale

#23 Valentine's Day
Disaster

#24 Field Trip to
Niagara Falls

#25 The Search for
Sunken Treasure

#26 The Mummy
with No Name

#27 The Christmas
Toy Factory

#28 Wedding
Crasher

#29 Down and Out
Down Under

#30 The Mouse Island
Marathon

#31 The Mysterious
Cheese Thief

Christmas Catastrophe

#32 Valley of the
Giant Skeletons

#33 Geronimo and the
Gold Medal Mystery

#34 Geronimo Stilton,
Secret Agent

#35 A Very Merry
Christmas

#36 Geronimo's
Valentine

#37 The Race Across
America

#38 A Fabumouse
School Adventure

#39 Singing Sensation

#40 The Karate Mouse

#41 Mighty Mount
Kilimanjaro

#42 The Peculiar
Pumpkin Thief

#43 I'm Not a
Supermouse!

#44 The Giant
Diamond Robbery

#45 Save the White
Whale!

#46 The Haunted
Castle

#47 Run for the Hills, Geronimo!

#48 The Mystery in Venice

#49 The Way of the Samurai

#50 This Hotel Is Haunted!

#51 The Enormouse Pearl Heist

#52 Mouse in Space!

#53 Rumble in the Jungle

#54 Get into Gear, Stilton!

#55 The Golden Statue Plot

#56 Flight of the Red Bandit

Special Edition!
The Hunt for the Golden Book

#57 The Stinky Cheese Vacation

#58 The Super Chef Contest

#59 Welcome to Moldy Manor

Special Edition!
The Hunt for the Curious Cheese

#60 The Treasure of Easter Island

#61 Mouse House Hunter

#62 Mouse Overboard!

Special Edition!
The Hunt for the Secret Papyrus

#63 The Cheese Experiment

#64 Magical Mission

#65 Bollywood Burglary

Special Edition!
The Hunt for the Hundredth Key

#66 Operation: Secret Recipe

#67 The Chocolate Chase

MEET
Geronimo Stiltonord

He is a mouseking — the Geronimo Stilton of the ancient far north! He lives with his brawny and brave clan in the village of Mouseborg. From sailing frozen waters to facing fiery dragons, every day is an adventure for the micekings!

#1 Attack of the Dragons

#2 The Famouse Fjord Race

#3 Pull the Dragon's Tooth!

#4 Stay Strong, Geronimo!

#5 The Mysterious Message

Meet
GERONIMO STILTONOOT

He is a cavemouse — Geronimo Stilton's ancient ancestor! He runs the stone newspaper in the prehistoric village of Old Mouse City. From dealing with dinosaurs to dodging meteorites, his life in the Stone Age is full of adventure!

#1 The Stone of Fire

#2 Watch Your Tail!

#3 Help, I'm in Hot Lava!

#4 The Fast and the Frozen

#5 The Great Mouse Race

#6 Don't Wake the Dinosaur!

#7 I'm a Scaredy-Mouse!

#8 Surfing for Secrets

#9 Get the Scoop, Geronimo!

#10 My Autosaurus Will Win!

#11 Sea Monster Surprise

#12 Paws Off the Pearl!

#13 The Smelly Search

#14 Shoo, Caveflies!

Don't miss any of my adventures in the Kingdom of Fantasy!

THE KINGDOM OF FANTASY

THE QUEST FOR PARADISE:
THE RETURN TO THE KINGDOM OF FANTASY

THE AMAZING VOYAGE:
THE THIRD ADVENTURE IN THE KINGDOM OF FANTASY

THE DRAGON PROPHECY:
THE FOURTH ADVENTURE IN THE KINGDOM OF FANTASY

THE VOLCANO OF FIRE:
THE FIFTH ADVENTURE IN THE KINGDOM OF FANTASY

THE SEARCH FOR TREASURE:
THE SIXTH ADVENTURE IN THE KINGDOM OF FANTASY

THE ENCHANTED CHARMS:
THE SEVENTH ADVENTURE IN THE KINGDOM OF FANTASY

THE PHOENIX OF DESTINY:
AN EPIC KINGDOM OF FANTASY ADVENTURE

THE HOUR OF MAGIC:
THE EIGHTH ADVENTURE IN THE KINGDOM OF FANTASY

THE WIZARD'S WAND:
THE NINTH ADVENTURE IN THE KINGDOM OF FANTASY

THE SHIP OF SECRETS:
THE TENTH ADVENTURE IN THE KINGDOM OF FANTASY

THE DRAGON OF FORTUNE:
AN EPIC KINGDOM OF FANTASY ADVENTURE

MouseStar I

The spaceship, home, and refuge of the spacemice!

MouseStar I
(exterior view)